Bantam Books in the Choose Your Own Adventure® Series
Ask your bookseller for the books you have missed

#1 THE CAVE OF TIME
#2 JOURNEY UNDER THE SEA
#3 BY BALLOON TO THE SAHARA
#4 SPACE AND BEYOND
#5 THE MYSTERY OF CHIMNEY ROCK
#6 YOUR CODE NAME IS JONAH
#7 THE THIRD PLANET FROM ALTAIR
#8 DEADWOOD CITY
#9 WHO KILLED HARLOWE THROMBEY?
#10 THE LOST JEWELS OF NABOOTI
#11 MYSTERY OF THE MAYA
#12 INSIDE UFO 54-40
#13 THE ABOMINABLE SNOWMAN
#14 THE FORBIDDEN CASTLE
#15 HOUSE OF DANGER
#16 SURVIVAL AT SEA
#17 THE RACE FOREVER
#18 UNDERGROUND KINGDOM
#19 SECRET OF THE PYRAMIDS
#20 ESCAPE
#21 HYPERSPACE
#22 SPACE PATROL
#23 THE LOST TRIBE
#24 LOST ON THE AMAZON
#25 PRISONER OF THE ANT PEOPLE
#26 THE PHANTOM SUBMARINE
#27 THE HORROR OF HIGH RIDGE
#28 MOUNTAIN SURVIVAL
#29 TROUBLE ON PLANET EARTH
#30 THE CURSE OF BATTERSLEA HALL
#31 VAMPIRE EXPRESS
#32 TREASURE DIVER

#33 THE DRAGONS' DEN
#34 THE MYSTERY OF THE HIGHLAND CREST
#35 JOURNEY TO STONEHENGE
#36 THE SECRET TREASURE OF TIBET
#37 WAR WITH THE EVIL POWER MASTER
#38 SABOTAGE
#39 SUPERCOMPUTER
#40 THE THRONE OF ZEUS
#41 SEARCH FOR THE MOUNTAIN GORILLAS
#42 THE MYSTERY OF ECHO LODGE
#43 GRAND CANYON ODYSSEY
#44 THE MYSTERY OF URA SENKE
#45 YOU ARE A SHARK
#46 THE DEADLY SHADOW
#47 OUTLAWS OF SHERWOOD FOREST
#48 SPY FOR GEORGE WASHINGTON
#49 DANGER AT ANCHOR MINE
#50 RETURN TO THE CAVE OF TIME
#51 THE MAGIC OF THE UNICORN
#52 GHOST HUNTER
#53 THE CASE OF THE SILK KING
#54 FOREST OF FEAR
#55 THE TRUMPET OF TERROR
#56 THE ENCHANTED KINGDOM
#57 THE ANTIMATTER FORMULA
#58 STATUE OF LIBERTY ADVENTURE
#59 TERROR ISLAND
#60 VANISHED!

CHOOSE YOUR OWN ADVENTURE® · 49

DANGER AT ANCHOR MINE

BY LOUISE MUNRO FOLEY

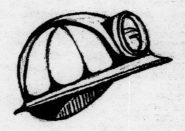

ILLUSTRATED BY LESLIE MORRILL

An Edward Packard Book

BANTAM BOOKS

TORONTO · NEW YORK · LONDON · SYDNEY · AUCKLAND

RL 4, IL age 10 and up

DANGER AT ANCHOR MINE
A Bantam Book / October 1985

CHOOSE YOUR OWN ADVENTURE® is a registered trademark of
*Bantam Books, Inc. Registered in U.S. Patent and Trademark
Office and elsewhere.*

Original conception of Edward Packard.

ISBN 0-553-25177-5

Published simultaneously in the United States and Canada

---

*Bantam Books are published by Bantam Books, Inc. Its trade-
mark, consisting of the words "Bantam Books" and the por-
trayal of a rooster, is Registered in U.S. Patent and Trademark
Office and in other countries. Marca Registrada. Bantam
Books, Inc., 666 Fifth Avenue, New York, New York 10103.*

PRINTED IN THE UNITED STATES OF AMERICA

O   0 9 8 7 6 5 4 3 2

This one is for Peggy Hutchison,
with love and admiration.

WARNING!!!

Do not read this book straight through from beginning to end. These pages contain many different adventures you may have while uncovering the secrets of the Anchor Mine. From time to time as you read along, you will be asked to make decisions and choices. Your choices may lead to success or disaster.

The adventures you have will be the result of your choices. After you make a choice, follow the instructions to see what happens to you next.

Think carefully before you make a move. Many have entered the mine and never left it. Will you claim the Anchor's gold? Or will Anchor Mine claim you?

Good luck!

Since your grandfather's death three years ago, you have spent the summers helping in your grandmother's store in a small Canadian mining town in northern Ontario. All the gold mines have been closed down for years. If it weren't for the tourists visiting the forests and lakes of the area, Kirkland would be a ghost town.

You've always liked the stories of the gold mines. Your grandfather worked at the Anchor Mine years ago, and he told you many tales about his adventures below ground. Just before the Anchor closed, your granddad and some of the other miners were paid in shares instead of money. They had hoped that they'd strike it rich, but the Anchor's gold petered out like all the rest.

Your grandmother still holds the Anchor stock. She says it's worthless, but you're not so sure. One day, when you're cleaning out the back shed at the store, you find a brown leather diary that belonged to your grandfather. You sit on the floor and begin to read:

Closed down #4 West after the accident yesterday. There could be a fortune in there. If only we had the key to Sam Carter's desk.

Does that mean there's still gold in the Anchor? you wonder.

Turn to page 2.

Your thinking is interrupted by loud voices coming from the store. You jump up and run in. Gram is standing by the cash register. A policeman is facing her. He's tall and heavy, and his bushy mustache moves up and down quickly as he talks.

"I'm warning you, Etta Mae! You pay your town taxes within ten days, or you're going to jail!"

Turn to page 5.

You shove the map and key into your pocket and hurry upstairs.

"Did you put everything back?" Miss Munson asks.

You nod as you dash out the door. There are several hours of daylight left. Enough to find the Piny Glen shaft! When you reach the main gates of the Anchor, you scale the fence and drop to the other side. Heading west, you walk for a long time over the uneven ground. Finally some structures come into view. They must be Piny Glen buildings. You pull out the map and study it. The Piny Glen shaft into #4 West must be somewhere near.

You scan the ground around you. Knowing there are rattlers in the area, you cautiously start pushing aside the brush. But you can find no sign of a shaft. Maybe the opening is inside a building, you think. You start to run toward the nearest structure.

You've gone only a few hundred yards when your foot plunges into a hole. A searing pain stabs at your ankle. For a moment you think you've found the shaft, but on closer examination you don't even have that to console you. It's just a hollow, washed out by spring rains and covered with overgrowth.

You inspect your ankle, which is starting to swell. When you try to stand, it won't support your weight.

You look around. The sun will soon set. You'll never be found out here in the dark, you think. You start to crawl toward the nearest building.

Turn to page 67.

"I've always paid my bills, Roderick, and you know it!" Gram snaps. "My payment's going to be a little late, that's all."

"You're already sixty days overdue!" the policeman roars.

"Money's been a bit tight," Gram says firmly. "The township will get theirs. I've had some . . . more important expenses."

"Eight hundred dollars in ten days, Etta Mae . . . or else!" he yells, stomping out the door.

"Who is he?" you ask Gram.

"Roderick Carter," she replies. "The town policeman."

"Do you really owe eight hundred dollars?" you ask.

"I had some unexpected expenses," Gram explains. "Don't worry about it. Roderick's like his uncle Sam. Just because they owned the Anchor, they think they own the town and everyone in it."

"His family owned the mine?" you ask.

Gram nods. "Your grandfather worked for Sam Carter. The man was crazy with greed. I get upset just talking about him."

Turn to page 7.

"You'll be even more sorry when you find out your driver's going straight to police headquarters," you say to Chuck.

"What are you talking about?" he asks warily.

"I hypnotized him while he was painting the truck," you say. "I put him in a trance and directed him by hypnotic suggestion."

Chuck glowers at you, but you can tell he's not totally discounting what you say. As Chuck nervously looks around the truck you sense Roderick shifting slightly. He's conscious!

"There aren't any windows," you say to Chuck. "You won't know where we're going until we get there."

"We'll see about that!" Chuck yells, grabbing his two-way radio. "Mac! Stop the truck! Open the back!"

Turn to page 110.

Your mind flashes back to the entry in the diary. Sam Carter's desk! If there's really a fortune in the Anchor and you could find it, you could pay off Gram's taxes. Maybe you should ask her to tell you more. But if she gets upset just talking about the Carters, she's not going to tell you much.

You might be wiser to deal directly with Roderick Carter.

If you ask Gram about Sam Carter,
turn to page 30.

If you go to find Roderick Carter,
turn to page 54.

The door at the top of the stairs slams as Miss Munson returns to the library.

You sit on the floor and open one of the Anchor boxes—technical reports, blueprints, engineering records. You feel as if you're wasting your time. Besides, if Roderick's already been through all this stuff, you know you're not going to find anything new about #4 West. You're closing the fourth Anchor box when a yellowed scrap of paper catches your attention. It's a receipt written to Sam Carter for five thousand dollars *"for 100 acres of land, previously known as the Piny Glen Mine, north-west of the town line; such agreement exclusive of structures thereon. . . ."*

Why would Sam Carter buy a mine that had already been worked? you wonder. Unless . . . You grab the box marked PINY GLEN and rummage through it, looking for a map. Your hunch is right! The Piny Glen butts up to the west side of the Anchor, and one shaft appears to be common to both. You squint to read the faded words: # 4 West! There's access to #4 West from the smaller mine!

Go on to the next page.

Excitedly you turn the box upside down and dump the contents on the floor. You can't believe what you see! Lying on the top of the clutter of papers is a key. A key that may fit a desk.

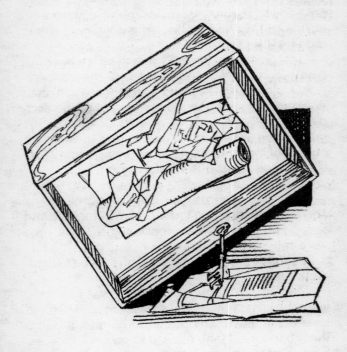

If you go to the Anchor office with the key, turn to page 12.

If you go to look for the Piny Glen shaft, turn to page 3.

"Annie's not dead!" you say to Mrs. Henry. "I saw her. I talked to her! Who is she anyway?"

"Annie Brynowski was an immigrant who came here from Poland with her husband, Joseph," Mrs. Henry says. "When Roderick's uncle—Sam Carter—found the new vein, Joseph sold almost everything they had to buy Anchor stock. Annie didn't want him to.

"Joseph was on the crew that went to check out Number Four West, on the day of the accident. Annie, along with the rest of us womenfolk, rushed down to the mine the minute we heard the accident whistle. Annie went sort of crazy. She grabbed an ax and forced her way on the elevator and went down to the level of the accident. Sam Carter tried to stop her but couldn't."

"And her husband died in the accident, right?"

"Yes," Mrs. Henry says. "But Annie took that ax and cut away burning timbers at the entrance and saved two men." Mrs. Henry sighs. "The men were my husband and your grandfather."

"Granddad?" you whisper. "She saved Granddad's life?"

"Yes," says Mrs. Henry. "But she wasn't treated like a heroine. Miners are superstitious. They believe that if a woman goes underground, it brings them bad luck. Many refused to go back to work. Sam Carter saw to it that Annie didn't get her husband's insurance money. Sam closed up Number Four West, and soon after the Anchor folded."

Turn to page 63.

You hear the cry for help again. The voice is coming from a long way into the tunnel. Voices get distorted underground, you realize, but it must be Roderick! Maybe he's injured.

Slowly you descend the ladder and inch through the blackness, feeling your way with your hands. The calls have stopped, and the silence is heavy. Was it your imagination? What if you should trigger the explosives, stumbling around there in the dark?

That's just a chance you'll have to take. Mrs. Henry was right about one thing. Every human life is precious. When you come to the bend in the tunnel, you stop.

"Where are you?" you call out. "I'm coming for you. Let me know where you are!"

Turn to page 15.

You shove the papers into the box and pocket the key.

"Did you put everything back?" Miss Munson asks accusingly.

"Oh, yes!" you reply, hurrying to the door. "Thanks!"

You run all the way to the Anchor. NO TRESPASS-ING signs are posted on the high chain-link fence. You scale the fence and drop to the other side, barely hitting the ground when you hear a car. It could be Roderick! You can't be seen here!

You run to the nearest building. A faded sign over the door says ANCHOR OFFICE. Inside there's an old desk and chair by one wall. Could that be Sam Carter's desk?

You walk to it and stoop down to try the key.

"Don't touch that desk!" says a gruff voice.

A short woman faces you. A miner's helmet al-most covers her gray hair, and in her hand she holds a short-handled ax.

"You're not one of the town kids," she says, staring at you.

"No," you reply. "I'm spending the summer with my grandmother. She runs the store."

"Town kids know better than to trespass," the woman growls. "They know what happened to that snoopy kid last summer."

Go on to the next page.

You remember the story. Some kid wandered onto mine property, fell down an open shaft, and died of a broken neck.

"Listen to Annie," she says, waving her ax. "This place is dangerous. Leave! And don't come back!"

Whoever Annie is, she's crazy, you think. You move toward the door, and turn to glance back inside. It's impossible! Annie has disappeared!

If you go back inside, turn to page 49.

If you decide to try the key some other time, turn to page 72.

You wait for an answer, but none comes.

You start walking. You come to a narrow point and trip over something. A person! Either dead— or unconscious. You feel the temple for a pulse. There is a very faint beat, and it's irregular. Is it Roderick? You lean over and feel for his metal badge. Yes! It *is* Roderick! He must have fallen and hit his head.

You know you're close to where the canary led you earlier. You can drag Roderick there and try to pull him up that rock and exit by the stream, or you can go back through the tunnel and up the ladder. Neither one will be easy.

If you go to the rock, turn to page 79.

If you go to the ladder, turn to page 38.

Everything's a risk, you think, placing your hands flat against the wooden door. Slowly you exert just enough pressure to slide it along the track. It inches open and you peer through the crack. You're staring straight into the barrel of a shotgun!

"Hold it right there!" says a familiar voice.

The door slides open farther.

"Gram! Put down that shotgun! What are you doing here?"

"Well, I could ask the same of you," Gram says. "Get in here and shut that door!" She puts down the shotgun and frowns at you.

But you hardly notice her anger. You're too busy looking beyond Gram at the people—three adults and three children—huddled in a back corner of the room. They look frightened.

"Ethel promised me she'd keep you upstairs!" Gram says.

"Well, she tried," you say. "But I saw the steps leading down here and decided I'd check it out."

"Where is she now?"

"Up there looking for Roderick." You lean forward and whisper, "Gram, who are those people?"

Go on to the next page.

"Guess there's not much point in keepin' it a secret from you. You'll just keep pesterin' me to find out," she says. "They're the Gomez family. Raul and María are the parents, Teresa is the grandmother, and Enrico and Ana and Francisco are the kids."

"Yeah, but what are they doing here? In the mine?"

Gram looks straight into your eyes. "Hiding," she says.

"Hiding from who?" you ask.

"The authorities," Gram says tersely.

Turn to page 82.

Without thinking, your hand reaches back to the diary in your back pocket. *Sam's desk!* Granddad wrote about wanting the key to Sam's desk. It must be connected to the gold, you think. If only you could find that key, maybe Gram would be able to pay off her taxes!

"What happened to the mine office?" you ask, trying to sound casual. "Did they sell off the furniture after Sam's death?"

"Far as I know," Gram replies, shaking her head, "it's the same as it was the day Sam died. They just closed up the door and walked away." She walks around the counter and frowns at you. "You stay away from the Anchor, hear me? Roderick's fining all trespassers!"

The bell on the store door jingles, and Gram goes to wait on her friend Mr. Grimble, the town gossip. You return to your sweeping, but your mind is racing.

Turn to page 25.

"I got the lantern from Annie," you tell Roderick.

"Annie who?" he asks suspiciously.

"She didn't tell me her last name," you answer. "She's an old lady and she wears a miner's helmet."

You see his face grow pale. "You're lying!" he says.

"I am not!"

"Where did you meet this Annie?" he asks.

"Down there," you reply, pointing to the tunnel exit.

"Is she still down there?" he asks, in a choked voice.

"Yes," you reply, wishing you hadn't said anything.

He leans forward and whispers. "Is there anything else . . . strange . . . about this Annie?"

"Well, she carries an ax," you say.

"Show me where she is," he demands, prodding you with his rifle.

You crawl over to the adit. Roderick follows you.

"Trespassers on Anchor property get fined," he says as you lead him through the tunnel. "I don't believe this Annie person exists. If she did, I'd know about her."

You scarcely hear his comments. Your mind is too busy trying to figure out a way to get out of this. You don't want to lead him to Annie. There's only one thing you can think of—divert him into exploring #4 West. But if #4 West is booby-trapped, that's a big risk for you.

Turn to page 46.

You circle the boulder cautiously. Behind it you find not Roderick, but a flight of stone steps leading down! You hurry down, counting as you go. When you get to the twenty-second step, you stop and sniff the air. You must be going a little crazy. You're sure you can smell coffee.

The steps jog around a corner, and you find yourself facing a heavy wooden door on rollers. Mrs. Henry said not to touch the walls. She didn't say anything about doors. You check the metal track on which the door sits. There are no wires, or anything that looks as if it may be a detonator. You hold the lantern up high so you can see the top track. It's impossible to tell in the shadowy light, but it looks as if there *may* be a wire up there.

Should you risk sliding the door along the track? Or should you go back up and search the tunnel Mrs. Henry assigned to you?

You sniff the air again. It *does* smell like coffee. Maybe Annie's behind the door. But Annie's supposed to be dead!

If you slide the door open, turn to page 16.

If you go back upstairs, turn to page 85.

"I'll go with you," you tell Mrs. Henry as she strides along.

"This is where I came out!" you say as you approach the adit.

"Oh, there's a better ladder in the one over here," she says. "There are several adits, some better than others." She stoops over and moves some brush aside. A metal ladder with wide steps descends into the ground. You follow her down the ladder.

"I hope he's still in the Chamber of Gold," she says. "I've been in there dozens of times. It's the tunnels that spoke out from it that I'm afraid of."

You stare at her. She's been in there dozens of times? Roderick didn't even know how to get into #4 West until you showed him.

"How come you're in the mine that often?" you ask.

Turn to page 28.

As soon as your captor rounds the back end of the truck you jump up and run for the elevator.

"Get that kid, Chuck!" the man in the suit yells.

Chuck isn't fast enough. You slam the metal door in his face and yank on the lever. But instead of going up, the elevator goes down. When it stops, you cautiously slide open the door.

"I told you to go and not return!" says a voice. Annie is standing there, holding a lantern. "Go back up. You'll never escape from here, but you might have a chance from the truck."

"They'll kill me," you say, wondering how she knows about the truck. "Chuck has a rifle."

"They won't fire the rifle underground," Annie says. "Randolph knows it's too dangerous. Now go back up. There's no way in or out from this level."

"Well, you got here!" you say. "And who's Randolph?" But even as you speak Annie disappears. You get back into the elevator. Chuck is waiting for you at the garage level.

"Let's go, kid!" He pushes you to the truck, boosts you into the back, and climbs in after you. The motor starts.

"Where are you taking me?" you ask as the truck speeds away from the mine.

Go on to the next page.

"Randolph says you and his cousin are going to have an accident." He points to Roderick, lying unconscious on the floor of the truck.

Cousin! That's why the man in the gray suit looked familiar. He's a half-size copy of Roderick Carter!

"Randolph's in for a surprise," you say. "Roderick knew his cousin was operating the hijacking ring out of the mine. He'd already called the police. Randolph's probably being booked right now!"

Turn to page 97.

Tomorrow is your day off. You could hike out to the Anchor and explore the office. The key to the desk may be hidden there! On the other hand from what Gram said, even the office could be dangerous. Maybe you ought to get some more information about #4 West and the accident before you go to the mine. The old newspapers on file in the library would surely have some stories about it.

If you decide to go directly to the Anchor, turn to page 32.

If you decide to go to the library first, turn to page 71.

26

"Annie's not dead!" you say to Mr. Grimble. "I saw her!"

"Just 'cause you saw her don't mean she ain't dead," he replies. "Annie Brynowski was the wife of a miner who was killed in the Number Four West cave-in, back in the thirties. She cursed the Anchor owner—that was Roderick's uncle, Sam Carter—and swore she'd get even."

You're about to ask him to tell you more about the accident when without warning you hear something that sounds like a sonic boom. The store starts to sway.

"Earthquake!" you say to Mr. Grimble in a frightened voice.

"Nope," he replies, as the second boom sounds. A couple of cans of soup fall from one of the shelves, and the hanging light fixture overhead sways like a pendulum. "Nope, those are blasts at the mine. I reckon it's Annie, gettin' even."

You look up at the swinging light and start to say something about superstition, but the words don't get past your lips. For there, perched on the metal shade, is a canary.

The End

Mrs. Henry looks away quickly, and you think she wishes she hadn't said so much. In fact, she has a guilty look.

"Here we are!" she says, avoiding your question. She looks around the empty chamber. "We'll have to track him. There are two main tunnels. You take this one . . ." She points to a narrow crevice. "I've been through it before. And I'll take the other. Carry that lantern. Walk slow. Keep your hands to your sides. If you find Roderick, tell him Ethel Henry's looking for him. We'll meet back here." Her voice softens. "Be careful," she says.

With that, Mrs. Henry sits down on the floor and slithers through the low opening. You are moving toward the narrow slit through which you're supposed to go when you think you hear a shuffling noise. Could Roderick be behind that boulder? Should you check on it? Maybe it was your imagination.

If you go through the opening to the tunnel, turn to page 105.

If you check behind the boulder, turn to page 20.

You must get the Gomez family out of their hiding place! You start down the passageway when the light appears again. Your heart starts to thump. It's scary now that you're alone.

"Get into the elevator," says a voice you've heard before. You turn quickly. The elevator is back on the floor of the grotto, and Annie is standing by it, beckoning to you.

"I have to get the Gomez family!" you say.

"They're safe." She pushes at you with her ax. "Get in."

Within minutes you're safely at the surface. Dr. Gomez is wrapping his shirt around Roderick's head wound. Annie must have rescued them too! Mrs. Henry takes the keys from Roderick's belt, and you and she hike over to get his car. She unlocks the main gates and drives through to pick up the rest of the group.

Turn to page 33.

"Did Granddad get along with Sam Carter?" you ask Gram.

"He and Sam respected each other until the accident in Number Four West."

That must be what the diary was talking about, you think. "What happened in Number Four West?" you ask.

"An explosion killed twelve miners," Gram answers. "Almost fourteen. Tom often said that Sam Carter set that blast."

"Why would he do that?" you ask, puzzled.

"Two possible reasons," Gram says. "To keep the men from knowing that there wasn't any gold in Number Four West. Or to keep them from knowing that there was."

"I don't get it."

"It's complicated," says Gram with a sigh. "You see, most of Sam's money was tied up in land. For several months he paid the miners in shares of Anchor stock. It was supposed to have been worth much more than their paychecks would have been. The men who helped open up Number Four West reported seeing rich veins in the loose quartz. They all thought they'd be millionaires."

Go on to the next page.

"What changed their thinking?" you ask.

"Rumors that Sam had salted Number Four West," Gram says.

"Salted?" you ask. "What's that?"

"Some said that Sam placed gold-bearing quartz in Number Four West to convince the miners that it was a rich strike. So they'd accept shares of stock instead of money for their labor."

Turn to page 44.

32

The next morning you tell Gram you're going to the ridge beyond the Anchor to pick blueberries.

She gives you a bucket and a lecture about staying off the property. "You put one foot on the Anchor, and I'll send you home on the next bus!" she says sternly.

Gram's threats don't bother you too much. She'll be busy in the store all day. Mr. Grimble has promised to come in and help, so she probably won't give you another thought.

When you reach the main gate at the mine, you grin at the NO TRESPASSING sign, drop your berry bucket, and scale the fence.

You figure that the office will be close to the gate, and go directly to the first building on your right. You're in luck! The door is ajar. You enter and wait for a few minutes until your eyes become accustomed to the dimly lit interior. The boarded-up windows allow little light to come in.

It's the office, all right! Two old bulletin boards are hanging on one wall, and over by another is a desk with a rack of mailboxes hanging behind it. Could that be Sam Carter's desk? you ask yourself.

Turn to page 35.

By morning, news of your adventure is all over town. Dozens of Gram's friends come to the store to meet the Gomez family and hear the story first-hand. You all become instant celebrities. A reporter from the newspaper comes to interview you, and a television station in a nearby town sends a crew to do a feature story. It's all wonderful—until Roderick shows up. His head is bandaged, but otherwise he's none the worse for the experience.

He stomps into the store and confronts Gram.

"I've got a warrant for your arrest, Etta Mae," he says. "And for them too." He points at the Gomez family. "They're here illegally, and you're harboring them!"

Suddenly the store becomes very quiet. And you become very angry. "If it weren't for Dr. Gomez and Gram," you say, "you'd be dead! We should have left you in the mine!"

Turn to page 70.

Your heart is pounding as you inch toward the desk. You may be on your way to finding a fortune! Nervously you go back to the door and peer outside to see if anyone is around. There's no sign of life on the property, and none on the road beyond. You check the office again, this time looking for wires. You don't see any.

Slowly you approach the desk again. You're within a few steps of it when something leaps out of the shadows. It's a dog! A big black dog. It positions itself between you and the desk, snarling.

Turn to page 104.

"I found the lantern over there," you say to Roderick, pointing off in the distance.

"What else did you find over there?" he asks.

"Nothing! Just some old buildings." You hope that *is* what's over there. All you want to do is mislead him so he doesn't notice the adit.

"Show me," Roderick says, yanking you to your feet.

You walk for a long time. Finally you come to some buildings by a grove of trees.

"That's where I found it!" you say, pointing to the grove. You turn to face Roderick as you speak, just in time to see a man creeping up behind him. He's carrying a rifle too.

"Look out!" you yell at Roderick, but the warning is too late.

Turn to page 42.

You scramble up the rock. The canary disappears through an opening at the top, and you slide through the small space after the bird. It's dark and cold, and you can't see what's below. On the other side of the rock you hear Roderick yelling.

"Where did you go? Where are you?"

The canary brushes past your ear and swoops down into the blackness. You take a deep breath and follow, sliding down, down, faster and faster. You must be falling down a shaft!

Turn to page 43.

38

Slowly you start dragging Roderick down the tunnel toward the ladder. He must be twice your weight. It takes all your energy to move him a few feet.

Within minutes you're exhausted. You stop to rest. Maybe you shouldn't be moving him, you think. Maybe he's injured. But you can't tell in the dark.

You run your hand over his head, but you don't feel any bumps, and you don't feel any blood. What could have happened?

You feel so comfortable just sitting there thinking. You doze off. Then something brushes against your face and wakes you. It's Annie's canary!

The canary flies back and forth. It seems to want you to follow. It's leading you to the ladder!

You struggle to your feet and grab Roderick's arms. You feel dizzy. Now you know what happened to Roderick! Tunnel gas!

Turn to page 40.

You're not going to let Gram go up to #4 West alone! There might be another explosion. You turn quickly to the Gomez family.

"Stay here!" you say, hoping they understand. They look frightened. You're frightened, too, but you can't think about that now. You run for the stairs and take them two at a time.

"Gram!" you yell, crawling around the rock in the chamber.

"In here!" Mrs. Henry's voice sounds far away. "Hurry!"

The voice is coming from behind the narrow opening in the wall. You slip through and hurry toward the sound. Gram and Mrs. Henry are dragging Roderick down the passageway. He is unconscious and bleeding from a head wound.

"We'll never get him back through that narrow opening," Gram says. "Your grandfather talked about a makeshift elevator in Number Four West. If I only knew where it was!"

Turn to page 47.

40

You must reach the adit. The air by the opening will be fresh. With a surge of strength you didn't know you had, you pull Roderick through the tunnel till you reach the foot of the ladder. The canary circles your head, lands lightly on your shoulder, and then flies up and out through the opening. Free and airborne!

"Good-bye!" you gasp after it. "Thank you!"

Turn to page 99.

The butt of the rifle crashes down on Roderick's head, and he slumps to the ground, unconscious. You sprint as fast as you can toward the trees, pausing only briefly when you notice a trail of dust ribboning across the mine property. As you watch, a silver tractor-trailer disappears right into the side of a hill!

Suddenly someone grabs you from behind and shoves you toward the nearest building. You wrench your head around to look at your captor. You don't recognize him. He pushes on a board nailed over the doorway, and a panel to the left slides open. "Move it," he says, shoving you inside.

The door slides closed behind you, and a sound like far-off thunder rumbles through the murky building. The floor trembles.

Turn to page 80.

The water is icy cold when you hit. Shocked by the impact, you surface and dog-paddle around until you get your bearings. Ahead you can see a faint light. You're in an underground channel. Is that daylight ahead? Trying not to panic, you swim against the current.

You exit in the forest that borders the mine, and climb the bank. All the way home you wait for the explosion, but none comes.

When you get back to the store, Gram is waiting on Mrs. Henry.

"Where have you been?" she yells. "Look at you! You're soaking wet! I've told you not to swim in the stream. There's a perfectly good pool at the park. Safer and warmer!"

You don't answer. Your mind is on Roderick and Annie and what's happening inside the mine.

"Here!" Gram says, shoving a bag of groceries at you. "Help Ethel home with her things." She frowns as you stand there shivering. "Or you can stay here and mind the store. But change your clothes. You'll catch a chill!"

If you go with Mrs. Henry, turn to page 50.

If you stay at the store, turn to page 90.

"They had scarcely opened up Number Four West," Gram continues, "when Sam closed it off and put the men to work in another section. Told them he was waiting for special machinery to come from the British Isles. They thought he was hiding something, so a group of them coming off shift one day decided to check Number Four West. The last two in only got as far as the entrance. They survived."

"Okay," you say to Gram. "I understand why Sam wanted to keep the men from knowing there *wasn't* any gold in there . . . but why would he want to keep them from knowing if there *was* gold?"

"Greed. He wanted it for himself. The other veins were petering out. Sam knew the Anchor was only a year or two away from closing. Your granddad thought that there *was* gold in Number Four West. He figured that Sam would offer to buy back the stock from the men, and then start working the mine again."

"But he never did?"

Go on to the next page.

"He didn't live long enough," Gram says. "Sam Carter went broke. Eventually went crazy. Kept seeing ghosts of the men who died in the explosion. Every day he went to the deserted mine office. One day he didn't come back. Shot himself in the head. The authorities found him sprawled across his desk."

"Why doesn't somebody open up the mine and investigate Number Four West?" you ask. "Maybe there *is* gold in there!"

"The entrance is blocked from the accident," Gram says. "And there may be other charges. Sam wired everything, even his desk. Didn't want anybody snooping in the Anchor records."

Turn to page 18.

You walk through the tunnel until you reach the four timbers.

"This way," you say to Roderick, turning into #4 West.

You walk slowly. Your heart pounds with each step you take, and you squint through the flickering lantern light for a better look at where you're walking. You could set off a charge at any moment. That would be the end of both of you!

Roderick follows slowly behind you. You can tell he's never been in this part of the mine before by the way he stops to examine the walls, holding the lantern close to the rock, looking for veins of gold.

Something brushes by your head, and you stop.

It's the canary! It lights on a ledge, flutters its wings, and moves on. It's trying to tell you something.

"What are you stopping for?" Roderick demands.

"The canary," you say, pointing to the bird.

"What canary?" Roderick mutters. "I don't see a canary!"

He stops to examine the wall again, but you keep moving, cautiously following the bird down the passageway.

You come to a large boulder that blocks your path. The bird perches on top of the rock, fluttering its wings. Are you supposed to follow?

Suddenly Roderick lets out a whoop. "It *is* gold!" he yells. He's far behind you in the passageway.

Turn to page 37.

She has barely spoken when you see a flickering light in the tunnel. Is it a gas devil—or Annie? You go to investigate. The light dances on the walls of a grotto and then swings up over your head. It seems to have no source. You look up. A rope is hooked around a rusted metal wheel. You jump up and grab the rope, pulling hand over hand. A primitive elevator descends from the darkness. Quickly you load Roderick in, pushing Gram and Mrs. Henry in after him.

"I'll stay and work the pulley," you say.

Gram protests, but you ignore her and pull on the rope. The elevator rises. Just when you think you have no more strength, you feel a thump. They've reached the top! They're safe! But what about you? And what about the Gomez family?

Turn to page 29.

No one's going to scare you off! Cautiously you reenter the office. That desk could mean a fortune! You hurry to it and try the key. Disappointment floods through you. The key is much too large.

Suddenly you hear a noise outside. Is crazy Annie back? You drop down and crawl under the desk. Instantly the floor gives way, and you start to slide! You stop with a thump on a wide ledge. You're inside a tunnel—and it's pitch-black!

Your breath comes in quick gasps, and you try to calm yourself. That's when you see it: a yellowish light moving toward you.

Granddad told you about seeing eerie lights underground. Maybe it's a pocket of mine gas—a gas devil! Miners dreaded them. A gas devil could easily explode or asphyxiate you. The light moves closer.

Turn to page 61.

"I'm not cold," you say to Gram. "I'll go with Mrs. Henry."

You pick up the groceries and follow Mrs. Henry outside.

"I live in that big gray house on the Anchor road," she says, "and I know where you've been. You've been at the mine, and you found the underground channel."

"I don't know what you're talking about," you mumble.

"Did Annie show you where the channel was?" she asks.

You almost drop the groceries. "Who's Annie?" you mutter.

"I'll tell you when we get inside," she says as you climb the steps. "Take the bags to the kitchen. I want to get a book."

Mrs. Henry goes into a room off the hall, and you go to the kitchen. You're putting the groceries on the counter when you freeze in place. Sitting on the windowsill is a yellow canary.

"Here, Birdie," Mrs. Henry calls from the doorway. She comes into the kitchen and puts a scrapbook on the table. The bird flies to her shoulder. Something strange is going on here!

Turn to page 52.

You stare in the direction Mrs. Henry was walking. The bobbing lantern is not in sight. Only black space spreads before you. The few stars in the sky offer little help, and you stumble and trip over brambles as you run to find her.

You peer into the darkness. It seems as if you've been running for a long time. You should be near the adit she entered, but you don't see it. Did you get turned around? You stop to get your bearings. You're sure you're running in the right direction. Or are you? Something rustles on the ground, and you jump aside.

A snake? Or a rat?

You must keep moving. Run!

Turn to page 60.

"Sit down," Mrs. Henry says. "This is the Anchor scrapbook."

You sit down and start turning the pages. Newspaper clippings from as far back as fifty years ago tell the Anchor story—its treasures, its tragedies, and its people.

SAM CARTER FINDS NEW VEIN ON WEST SIDE

Special equipment has been ordered from a British firm to work the new vein, #4 West. Excitement is high among the miners, as many hold Anchor stock. This could be the richest vein yet.

You turn the page and read the headline:

HEROINE OF MINE CAVE-IN DIES IN FIRE

You're staring at a picture of Annie.

Turn to page 10.

You wait until Gram gets into a conversation with Mr. Grimble, the town gossip, and then sneak out to the street.

"Where's the policeman's office?" you ask a lady going by.

"Beside the barbershop," she says, pointing across the street.

You hurry across and look in the window. Roderick Carter is sitting with his feet up on a messy desk. You open the door.

"What d'you want, kid?" Roderick asks.

"I want to talk to you," you say, trying to sound confident.

"If it's about your grandmother's taxes, forget it. She either pays up or she goes to jail. Or she can sell the store. That's an option. I just collect for the township."

"I have another option," you say. "It's your uncle's desk."

Roderick swings his feet down and leans forward to stare at you. "What do you know about my uncle's desk?" he asks.

Go on to the next page.

"I found a diary that belonged to my grandfather," you say. "It has some information I think you'd like to have."

"You little twerp," Roderick says through tight lips. "How do I know you're not lying? Be more specific."

You swallow hard. You can't back down now.

"It's about Number Four West," you say. "There's a fortune in there."

"How much do you want?" Roderick asks.

"I want half of everything," you say, staring at him.

Turn to page 87.

"I'll go as far as the adit," you tell Mrs. Henry as you follow her across Anchor property. "It's right over here." The very thought of going back into the mine sends chills through your body.

"I'm not going down that adit," Mrs. Henry says, grinning. "There's one with a better ladder farther along. You wait here."

"You mean, there's another opening?" you ask.

"There are many old shafts in the Piny Glen portion of the Anchor," she tells you. "You have to be careful where you walk."

It's now dark, and as you watch her go the light of her lantern, bobbing with each step she takes, casts an eerie glow on the landscape. Heart pounding, you wait in the quiet darkness for what seems like an eternity. You try to occupy your mind with happy thoughts, but the frightening events of the day won't allow that. And the idea keeps creeping into your head that somewhere down this tunnel there's another human being who's in danger. For you don't expect Roderick will get out of this alive.

What if the adit Mrs. Henry takes doesn't lead her to Roderick? After all, this is the tunnel where you left him. Maybe you should go down the ladder and look for him.

The thought has scarcely passed through your head when you hear a cry for help from somewhere far down inside the tunnel.

If you respond to the cry for help, turn to page 11.

If you go to find Mrs. Henry, turn to page 51.

"Remember," you warn Chuck as you start climbing. "We're partners. I get fifty percent!"

Chuck nods. "Pull over, Mac," he says into the radio.

"You having problems back there, Chuck?" Mac asks.

"No!" Chuck says excitedly. "No problems."

You feel the truck gear down. You know that you're going to have to hurry. You know Mac is going to check in the back.

"Did you find the key?" Chuck yells as you crawl around the boxes.

"Yes!" you say. Chuck comes closer and looks up at you.

This is your chance. Quickly you shove the top carton down on him. It knocks him off balance, and you push off a second and a third. The fourth one cracks him on the side of the head, and Chuck lands in a heap and lies quiet on the floor of the truck.

You're not safe yet. The truck has stopped, and you can hear Mac unlocking the rear door. You jump down and grab Chuck's rifle. When the door swings open, you fire a shot in the air, and Mac takes off on the run.

Then you sit down to wait, keeping one eye on the open door and the other on the two unconscious men in the truck. Within ten minutes the police car pulls up beside the illegally parked rig.

Turn to page 65.

You glance at the rifle again. You have to plan this carefully. You wait till you feel the big truck gear down. The driver must be getting ready to turn around.

Chuck is pacing up and down the aisle between the cartons. When he's at the farthest spot from the rifle, you make your move. As quick as an arrow, you leap for the weapon. But Chuck moves just as fast. You grab the rifle and Chuck grabs you. With one arm holding you off the floor he tries to wrestle the rifle from your grasp. It fires . . . and then fires again.

Turn to page 64.

You're so alone out there. Mrs. Henry said there were many old shafts. You should probably be more careful. Or less cowardly.

But the realization comes too late. Your foot plunges into an open shaft.

You would have been safer going back into the mine with Mrs. Henry or down the adit to find Roderick. They got out alive.

Searchers find you two days later, dead of a broken neck.

The End

It's Annie! In one hand she holds the ax; in the other a lantern. She motions for you to follow, and you move slowly along the ledge until you reach a narrow opening.

You step into a cavernous room, outfitted with a mattress and a small metal stove. The walls are shored up with heavy timbers.

"You live here!" you say. "Who are you?"

"Your grandfather was my friend," she replies. "And no one must find out that I live here."

"Is this Number Four West?" you ask apprehensively.

"We are next to one part of it," she replies.

A bird swoops by your head and you duck.

"Here, Birdie," Annie calls. The canary flies to her shoulder.

Grandfather talked about taking birds below ground. If a bird died, the miners knew that air was impure, and they would return to the surface.

Turn to page 76.

As you sit, thinking about how you can escape the hijackers, two men carry Roderick in and dump him inside the truck.

"Thought you could fool Randolph Carter, didn't you?" growls a voice. "I was watching you. I knew you were in cahoots with Roderick the minute you walked into the library."

"But I'm not!" you protest. But it's no use.

"Sam Carter cheated my father—his own brother—out of his share of the mine profits. But I'm having the last laugh! My operation is making more money than the mine ever would have produced in gold!" He nods to the man who brought you in. "Take care of them, Chuck!"

Turn to page 68.

"Gram says Number Four West is booby-trapped," you tell Mrs. Henry. "So does Annie."

"Yes, I think it is too," she replies.

"Does Roderick know that?" you ask.

"It doesn't matter," says Mrs. Henry. "Annie wouldn't let anyone go in there. Number Four West is sealed off."

"But it's not!" you tell her. "I took Roderick in there. Through an adit. He's there right now!"

Mrs. Henry sighs. "You must have gone in through the Piny Glen," she says, slowly getting up from the table. "Well, we'd better go and rescue him before he blows himself up."

"What?" you yell. "Why?"

"Because every human life is precious. Even Roderick's."

Turn to page 69.

You're barely aware of the stains appearing on the cartons on the opposite side of the truck until you feel Chuck slip. He lurches forward, and then jerks back to keep from falling. Pools of shampoo are forming on the floor of the van! The shots have pierced the plastic bottles.

Chuck slips again. This time you give him an assist. You jerk sideways as he holds you, and he goes down with a crash. His head hits the metal floor. He moans once and then lies still.

The air brakes scream as the driver pulls over to the side of the road. He's heard the shots and the scuffle! You'd better be ready to defend yourself when he opens those back doors. You look at the rifle and decide against it. You don't want to kill anyone. You just want to get out of there.

You rip into a carton and grab one of the plastic shampoo bottles. You kneel by the door. As it swings open you squeeze the bottle, squirting shampoo right into the face that appears.

Turn to page 94.

"I don't care if you did help catch the hijackers," Gram yells when you get back to the store. "You're grounded! If I catch you near Anchor property again, I'll send you home!"

"Yes'm," you say meekly as your fingers tighten around the key in your pocket. But already you're making plans. Next Monday is your day off, and you can't wait to get to C. R. Munson's desk. After all, Gram didn't say anything about going to the Piny Glen.

The End

You drag yourself up the wooden steps and push the door open. The room is empty except for an old desk shoved into a corner. On one wall is a drab mural in greens and browns—a forest scene that looks like the wooded areas of the province. Above the mural, in old-fashioned gold-and-black lettering, is the inscription THE PINY GLEN MINE, C. R. MUNSON, OWNER.

You sit with your back against the opposite wall and stare at the mural. The late-afternoon sun is streaming in through the window behind you, casting golden lights on the faded painting—dancing golden lights that make you squint. Your ankle is throbbing. You close your eyes and fall asleep.

Turn to page 73.

68

Chuck shoves you to the rear of the truck and climbs in after you. The back door slams shut and the engine starts. Roderick is slumped beside a packing case, and you sit down beside him. Chuck props his rifle against a crate and speaks into a two-way radio.

"Take the back road and pick up the highway at Prentice," he tells the driver. "We'll dump the cargo north of the bridge."

You sit very still and stare at Chuck.

"What are you staring at?" he growls.

"You," you reply. "You don't know who I am, do you?"

"You're a friend of his," Chuck snaps, motioning at Roderick.

"I hardly know him," you say. "Don't you recognize me? I'm the Child Hypnotist. I've performed in every major city in Canada and the United States. You must have heard about me!"

"Sorry," Chuck replies in a bored voice.

Turn to page 6.

Mrs. Henry leaves the kitchen and comes back in a few minutes wearing overalls and sturdy lace-up boots. On her head is a miner's hat, and she's carrying a lantern and an ax.

"Come on, Birdie!" She whistles once, and the canary flies to her shoulder. She nods to you. "I'm ready. Let's go!"

You follow her out the door and across the road to the Anchor property. Mrs. Henry walks about a hundred feet past the main gates and carefully unhitches a section of fence, climbs through, and beckons for you to follow. Once inside she replaces the section. The chain links interlock so perfectly that no one would ever know.

You sense that she must have done this many times before.

"It's dangerous," Mrs. Henry says. "I'd like to have you with me in case Roderick's unconscious. But it's up to you. Would you rather wait here?"

If you decide to go with Mrs. Henry, turn to page 22.

If you decide to wait above ground, turn to page 56.

Roderick sputters at your outburst and turns his attention to you. "I'll arrest you, too, you smart-mouth kid!" he roars.

You gulp and look beyond him. Mrs. Henry winks at you and nods and smiles. What's she trying to tell you? Keep it up?

"You're nothing but a big bully!" you yell at Roderick.

Over his shoulder you can see Mrs. Henry and the customers quietly ushering the Gomez family out the back door.

"You don't care a thing about other people!" you holler. "All you care about is yourself—and the gold in the Anchor!"

Turn to page 74.

Early the next morning you go to the town's small library. A sign on the librarian's desk says MISS MUNSON. There's not another soul in the place.

"Yes?" she asks.

"I'm visiting here," you say casually, just the way you rehearsed it on the way over. "I'm curious about that big mine on the north side of town. Do you have any information about it?"

"The Anchor? We have some boxes of papers in the basement. Only one who ever looks at them is Roderick Carter." She peers at you over her spectacles. "You a Carter?"

"No," you reply. "Could I see the material?"

"I suppose," she answers grudgingly. "But it's not cataloged. Follow me," she says, leading you to a stairway.

You follow Miss Munson downstairs, into a small room in the basement. The overhead lightbulb casts shadows on the cardboard boxes that are piled on the floor.

"This is the mining section," she explains. "We have stuff on the Royal and the Lake Shore and the Piny Glen. And those boxes over there are all Anchor material. Now, mind you put everything back in the right cartons!" she warns.

"I've never heard of the Piny Glen," you say.

"The Piny Glen is the oldest mine in the township," Miss Munson says. "They closed it about the turn of the century. It was being worked before they ever put a machine on Anchor land!"

Turn to page 8.

That woman disappeared into thin air! You don't know if the Anchor is dangerous, but Annie and her ax could be!

You wonder if she had anything to do with the death of that kid last summer. You start to run, turning around just once to see if Annie's following.

That's your mistake. As you turn, your foot plunges into a hole, and you plummet down to the bottom of an open shaft.

Gingerly you get to your feet and carefully flex your legs, first one and then the other. You're lucky. No broken bones.

You look up. It's a long way to the ground above, and the rotting wood on the sides won't hold your weight. You sit down on the leaf-strewn ground to think. You're utterly alone! There must be some way out of this.

That's when you hear it. The unmistakable clicking sound of a rattler.

You were wrong on two counts. You're not alone, and you're not lucky. And Annie—whoever she is—was right. The Anchor is dangerous.

Maybe next summer some kid will remember the story about you and stay away from the mine.

The End

When you wake, you're in a hospital bed. Gram is sitting beside you.

"How did you find me?" you ask.

"Margaret Munson said you'd been to the library. She could tell that you'd been in the Piny Glen box."

"How could she tell?"

"She knows when anyone looks through her father's papers!"

"I wondered if they were related," you say. "His name was on the wall. Owner of the Piny Glen Mine."

"A sad story," Gram says. "Charley Munson's wife was ill for a long time. He called in specialists and sent her to an overseas clinic, where she eventually died. Soon after, Charley ran out of money to operate the mine. Some of his equipment broke down, and he couldn't afford to have it repaired. Sam Carter offered to buy the Piny Glen. He paid Charley almost nothing for it."

"What happened to Charley?" you ask.

Turn to page 102.

Gram is the last one to leave. The minute she's out the door, a car motor starts. And another and another. By the time Roderick catches on, it's too late. A caravan of cars and pickups and campers is moving down Main Street toward the highway. There's no way to tell which car is carrying the Gomez family.

"You can't arrest them all," you say to Roderick, trying not to smile.

He sputters as he watches them go. The street is deserted except for one van, rounding the corner. The television crew!

A man jumps out of the van and holds up a mike for Roderick.

"Would you like to give us a statement on the refugee family?"

"No comment," Roderick growls. "I don't know anything about a refugee family." He stomps down the street toward his office.

"There goes your story," you say, pointing after the caravan.

"Well, let's catch up with it!" the TV man says. "Hop in! Which car do you think they're in?"

You smile. "The one with the light flickering over the roof," you tell him.

The End

Maybe Annie knows what Granddad's diary meant, you think.

"What's the big secret in the desk?" you ask her.

"I think there's a map in the desk," she replies, "that shows where Sam Carter hid the charges in Number Four West."

"Then Number Four West *is* booby-trapped," you say.

"Yes, and so is the desk. Sam was a munitions expert."

You look at this strange old lady and frown. Can you trust what she's telling you, or is she trying to scare you off?

Turn to page 81.

You feel as if you ought to go with Gram to look for Mrs. Henry, but you really don't want to. You're beginning to think those two old ladies are crazy anyway—prowling around a mine wired with explosives, and hiding illegal aliens! You look across the room at the Gomez family.

They're huddled in a little cluster by the cots Gram has set up for them. A pot of coffee sits on a small stove against a wall. Canned goods are stacked on the floor by two water bottles.

Raul Gomez looks at you and starts to speak when another explosion jars the room.

It's time to get out of there! You whirl around, reaching the door just in time to see an avalanche of rock sliding down the stone steps. It's the last thing you remember.

Turn to page 106.

You hitch your arms under Roderick's armpits and struggle toward the rock, starting and stopping many times. Your whole body feels weary— as if you haven't slept for days—and your breath comes in short, shallow pants.

When you reach the rock, you're not at all sure you're going to make your goal. You feel the steep side for toeholds, and your fingers close around something soft. Soft and feathery!

It's Annie's canary. And it's dead.

Turn to page 86.

80

The man pushes you across the room. It's bare except for a forest-scene mural painted across one wall. Above the painting, in old-fashioned gold-and-black lettering, is the sign:

THE PINY GLEN MINE, C. R. MUNSON, OWNER

"Keep movin', kid," says the man, shoving you into an old cagelike elevator. He slides the barred door shut and pulls on a lever. Slowly the elevator begins to descend. You're going down one of the Piny Glen shafts!

The elevator stops with a thump. You're inside a huge underground garage! The silver tractor-trailer is parked, and two men are spray-painting it yellow. This must be a hijacking ring!

Turn to page 88.

"Do you own Anchor stock the way my gram does?" you ask.

"Yes, but it's worthless." Annie gets up. "You must leave now. And you must never return. I'll show you how to get to ground level."

"Just tell me," you say. "I can find my way out."

"Take the lantern, then. Follow the ledge to the left, and when you come to the fourth timber pointing west, turn right. That tunnel becomes an adit."

"An adit?"

"A tunnel that surfaces in daylight," Annie explains.

You wave at her halfheartedly as you leave. "Fourth timber pointing west," you whisper to yourself. "Number Four West!"

If you decide to turn right at the fourth timber and leave, turn to page 93.

If you decide to follow the ledge and enter #4 West, turn to page 96.

"What did they do?" you ask.

"They didn't do anything wrong," Gram says. "Their country is ruled by a dictator. Raul and María are doctors. They would have been put to death if they had stayed."

"Why?"

"They were caught treating wounded guerrillas," Gram explains. "Their clinic was burned, and two nurses were murdered."

"This is why you can't pay your taxes, isn't it?" you ask. "You're spending your money on Latin American refugees!"

"Yes," Gram says softly. "My sister in Arizona works with a group that offers them protection. She asked me to take them in."

"You could go to jail!" you say. "It's illegal! It's wrong!"

"It's illegal . . . but I don't think it's wrong," Gram says firmly. "It's worth the risk."

"They can't live here in the mine forever!" you point out.

"My goodness, no!" Gram replies. "They'll move on in a week."

"And others will move in," you say. "That's why Mrs. Henry didn't want Roderick snooping around in the mine."

Go on to the next page.

Gram nods. "Ethel and I hope that eventually they'll all get papers to make them legal residents of this country."

"Where do they go from here?" you ask.

"To another sanctuary," Gram says. "It's like the Underground Railroad in the times of slavery. Come and meet them."

But before you can move, an explosion shakes the room.

"Ethel!" Gram says fearfully. "Stay here!"

She grabs a lantern and hurries through the sliding door.

If you stay in the room, turn to page 77.

If you follow Gram to investigate, turn to page 39.

You're not going to risk opening the wooden door. You turn around and run back up the stairs.

It's hard getting up the back side of the boulder, and you keep losing your grip and sliding back down. Finally you put your arms around the boulder and dig the toe of your tennis shoe into a tiny niche in the rock. Then you place your other foot flat against the wall to give you some leverage.

You take a deep breath and push as hard as you can against the wall. The explosion is heard all over town.

How were you to know? Mrs. Henry didn't tell you not to touch the walls with your feet.

The End

Tears trickle down your cheeks. You cry for the bird and for Roderick and for yourself, for you know what your fate is.

Roderick knew too. He must have found the dead bird on the rock and realized the air was bad in the tunnel. He tried to reach the adit, but there wasn't enough oxygen to keep him going. You feel again for the pulse in his temple. There is none. You lay the canary on his chest and start crawling back down the tunnel.

Searchers find your body the next day, and the adit is sealed off as a safety measure. But no one goes to the end of the tunnel. The other body is never found. And the infamous #4 West becomes a tomb for Roderick and his fictitious fortune.

The End

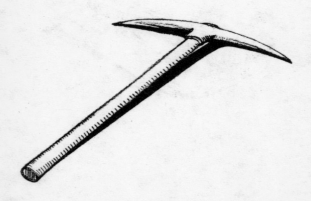

Roderick leans back in the chair, and a slow smile creeps across his face. "Sure, kid," he says.

"I want it in writing!" you say, puzzled by his reaction.

"Of course," he replies. He pulls a notepad from the drawer and starts to write. He signs his name with a flourish, tears the sheet off, and hands it to you. "Go get the diary," he says.

You read what he's written before you leave. It sounds legal. You tuck the paper in your pocket and run back to the store.

"Gram!" you yell, waving the paper. "We're going to be rich! You can pay your taxes and you won't go to jail. Look!"

Turn to page 95.

"Hurry it up!" a voice yells. "I want that rig on the road by dark. With two passengers!"

You turn to see who's giving the orders. It's a small man in a gray suit. He looks vaguely familiar, but you can't place him.

The man who captured you shoves you into a chair and walks around the truck to inspect the paint job.

This may be your only chance to escape. Should you make a run for the elevator? Or wait and try to escape from the truck?

If you decide to make a run for the elevator,
turn to page 23.

If you wait to escape from the truck,
turn to page 62.

"I'll stay here and mind the store," you say to Gram. "You and Mrs. Henry can visit on the way to her place."

"Well, go and get out of those wet things before we leave."

When you come back, Mr. Grimble is leaning on the counter.

"Cyrus will stay and help you," Gram says.

Usually you're not overjoyed to have Mr. Grimble around. He talks too much, and he's always bragging about the "good old days." But today that might be helpful. You'd really like to know who Annie is and why Roderick was frightened when you mentioned her.

"Been over to the Anchor, huh?" Mr. Grimble says to you as Mrs. Henry and Gram leave. "Saw you climbing the fence."

"I looked around the office," you say, trying to sound casual.

"And what did you see?" Mr. Grimble asks.

"Not much," you reply. "I met a woman named Annie."

You watch him for a reaction. He slowly raises his peaked cap and scratches his head. But his eyes narrow and his hand shakes.

Go on to the next page.

"Annie?" he repeats. "Annie who?"

"I thought you'd be able to tell me," you say.

"What did she look like?" he asks.

As you describe Annie Mr. Grimble's face becomes solemn.

"I saw Roderick over there too," you say. "And when I told him about Annie, he looked frightened."

"Yup," says Mr. Grimble, nodding. "He should be. Annie's been dead for ten years."

Turn to page 26.

You reach the fourth timber pointing west and turn right.

"I'll be back," you say with a grin as you rap your knuckles against it. "Just as soon as I can find that desk key."

You walk for a long time. When you notice the oil in the lantern is getting low, you quicken your pace. Finally you see a glimmer of light ahead. Daylight! The tunnel slopes sharply upward now, and you climb up, breathing hard. It will be good to get out into the fresh air.

You pull yourself through the opening and stretch out on the ground, exhausted.

Suddenly you're aware of a person near you.

"Okay, kid!" booms a voice. "Where did you get that lantern?"

You look up, startled. It's Roderick, and he's holding a rifle. Are you going to tell him the truth? Annie said no one must know that she lives down there. And she did say she was your grandfather's friend. Maybe you should lie.

If you tell Roderick the truth, turn to page 19.

If you lie to protect Annie, turn to page 36.

"Cut that out!" the man yells, throwing his arm up to protect his eyes.

He grabs your arm and yanks you out of the truck. It's not the driver at all, but a uniformed Provincial policeman. Parked behind the truck is the patrol car. You can hear his partner up at the cab questioning the driver about an illegal turn.

"Boy, am I glad to see you!" you say.

"I wouldn't have guessed it," says the policeman, wiping the shampoo from his face. He peers into the truck. "Who are they?" he asks, pointing to Roderick and Chuck.

"It's a long story," you answer.

They take you to headquarters in a nearby town, where you give your statement. The police have been after the hijacking ring for six months but didn't suspect they were operating out of the mine.

You tell them everything, except about Annie. You plan to investigate that mystery yourself. Who is she? And why is she living in the mine? you wonder.

Turn to page 101.

Gram takes the paper from your hand, and Mr. Grimble reads over her shoulder. Then she looks up at you and shakes her head.

"Roderick's welcome to read that diary for nothing," she says.

"But there's a secret in there!" you say. "About Sam Carter's desk and a key and a fortune!"

"Some secret," Mr. Grimble says, biting back a smile.

"You mean, it . . . isn't a secret?" you say hesitantly.

"No," Gram says. "That story's been going around town for thirty years. There's supposed to be a map in the desk—and the desk is supposed to be booby-trapped."

She sees your disappointment and reaches over to pat your hand. "Thanks for trying to help," she says. "But you learned something. There's no quick way to a fortune. Now, take that diary to Roderick and get back here and finish cleaning the shed!"

The End

You cautiously move along the ledge until you see the timbers pointing west. You count them off and then hold the old lantern up by the fourth one. A narrow tunnel winds behind it. You can't just leave now!

Your heart is hammering. There could be a fortune in there! you think. Surely the charges wouldn't be this close to the main tunnel. A quick look won't hurt.

You hold the lantern down so you can see where you're walking, and turn left. You move very carefully. Directly ahead a loaded gondola sits on a cross-track, blocking your way. Your lantern flashes on white quartz, and you see a glimmer of yellow. Could it be gold? You hurry toward the gondola.

Turn to page 111.

"You're lying!" Chuck says.

"I'm *not* lying!" you tell him. "Roderick had already called. What do you think he was doing there? The police are on their way to the Piny Glen!"

"No!" Chuck says, in a whisper. "No!"

"If you kill us, they'll know exactly who did it," you continue. "If you're smart, you'll stop this rig and let us off."

Chuck reaches for the two-way radio. Your trick is working!

"Turn around," Chuck tells the driver. "We're going back."

Your heart sinks. It *didn't* work! If you go back to the garage now, he'll know you were lying. The police won't be there, and you'll be killed for sure! You're going to have to stop this truck, but how? You glance at Roderick. He's still unconscious.

Chuck's rifle is leaning against some cartons. If you can get the weapon, maybe you can prevent the truck from turning back.

You look at the cartons that are stacked to the roof of the truck, and sigh in disgust. SOF'CURL SHAMPOO . . . SOF'CURL CONDITIONER . . . SOF'CURL RINSE. . . . If it was canned goods, you'd at least have something heavy to throw. But a truck full of beauty products doesn't offer much help. Maybe you could make up another lie to stop them from going back to the mine. It's that or the rifle.

If you grab Chuck's rifle, turn to page 58.

*If you make up another lie,
go on to the next page.*

"If you go to the Piny Glen," you tell Chuck, "you're going to get arrested right along with Randolph."

"Randolph's too smart to get arrested," he says. "He can hide the whole operation on another level in five minutes."

"Well, he wasn't smart enough to pick up the fortune I found in the library," you tell him.

Chuck glowers at you. "What do you mean?"

"I mean that I found the key."

"What key?" Chuck asks suspiciously.

"Sam Carter's desk key. I found it this morning."

You pull the key from your pocket, and Chuck snatches it from your hand, inspects it closely, and starts to laugh.

"It's the stupid key from the Piny Glen box," he says, angrily hurling it up into the stacks of cartons. "We tried that in Sam Carter's desk years ago. It's way too big!"

Turn to page 107.

You suck in big gulps of fresh air. Roderick is regaining consciousness. You help him up the ladder, and you both collapse on the ground.

"I apologize, kid," he says gruffly. "You saved my life. I thought when I found the dead bird that I was done. Thank you."

Dead bird? You start to speak and then stop. Who knows? After all, Annie's supposed to be dead too.

You do know one thing. You're grateful to be alive.

The End

The police give you a ride back to the store. Gram is not pleased with you. The next morning she puts you to work.

"I don't care if you did help uncover the hijackers," she says. "Around here you're still the hired help. Unpack those cartons and fill up the shelves."

You spend the next hour lining up bottles of Sof'Curl shampoo . . . Sof'Curl conditioner . . . and Sof'Curl rinse.

The End

"Charley Munson went kind of crazy," Gram tells you. "He kept saying he was rich, that he had a fortune in gold. Even on his deathbed he told Margaret that he'd leave her a place walled in gold. Of course, nobody believed him."

Your mind darts back to the gold specks flickering on the mural in the late-afternoon sun. "I believe him," you say. "Gram, you better call Margaret Munson. I think I have a surprise for her."

It takes six weeks for your broken ankle to heal, but you don't mind much. You've become something of a celebrity in town. Margaret Munson gives you a large reward for your discovery, and you're able to pay off Gram's taxes. You don't have a chance to do any more sleuthing on the mine property, but you can wait till next year.

One gold strike a summer is enough for you.

The End

You start to speak to the dog, but the words catch in your throat. You stretch out your hand, and the growl becomes more ferocious. You can't be stopped now! You're within a few feet of your goal. Then another thought occurs to you. The dog looks well fed. It's not a stray, you think. What if the owner is around? What if the dog belongs to Roderick?

Frightened and disappointed, you back away from the desk and out the door. You'll have to come back some other time. You climb the fence, pick up your bucket, and head for the ridge. You're walking along the road when you hear a car behind you.

"Going to pick some berries, I see," the driver yells.

It's Roderick. The dog must have been his!

"I'll give you a lift to the ridge," he says. "Climb in."

"No, thanks," you mumble. "I need the exercise." You breathe with relief as he shrugs and drives off.

Turn to page 108.

You can check behind the boulder later. Right now you'd better follow Mrs. Henry's directions. You slide through the narrow crevice and hold up the lantern to get your bearings. You're in a main tunnel, but this one seems to have several passageways leading off to the sides. You start with the first one. It's short and dead-ends into a wall of rock. The second and the third are no better, but the fourth tunnel curves around, and from the far end you can hear tapping noises. You hurry down its length and round the corner.

Roderick is on his hands and knees on the floor, tapping at the wall with the butt of his rifle.

"Don't!" you yell at him. "You could set off a charge!"

He turns and smirks at you. "I'll take that chance," he says. "There's enough gold in here to keep me rich for the rest of my life!"

"Ethel Henry says you're to come with me!" you yell at him.

"Ethel Henry can go jump down a shaft," Roderick says. He picks up his rifle and taps the wall again.

Turn to page 113.

When you come to, you're on the ground, looking up at the stars. Your head hurts, and your eyes have trouble focusing. You struggle to sit up, but someone holds you down.

"Stay still," Gram says. "Ethel's gone home to call an ambulance."

"Is everyone. . . ?" You're too groggy to finish the sentence.

"Everyone's safe," Gram says. "Raul and María pulled you out. They saved Roderick too. He would have bled to death."

You're aware of another person lying beside you. Roderick!

"Why?" you ask. "He'll turn them in. You too!"

"Human life is precious," Gram says, holding your hand. "It's worth the risk."

The End

The bluff didn't work. You try not to let your disappointment show as your mind races.

"Wrong desk!" you blurt out. "When Sam Carter bought the Piny Glen, C. R. Munson's desk became Sam Carter's desk. The agreement didn't say anything about the furniture."

Chuck gasps. "That's right!" he says. "Where's that key?"

"You threw it away," you say. "Up on those cartons. I'll climb up and find it, but I want fifty percent of what's in the desk. Tell the driver to pull over."

Chuck reaches for his two-way radio.

Turn to page 57.

That afternoon, when you get back to the store with the blueberries, Gram asks you to help Mr. Grimble carry some groceries to his truck. You pick up a box and follow the elderly man outside.

"Just put 'em in the back," he tells you.

You lean over the tailgate to put in the groceries and almost drop them. Lying curled up in one corner, lazily watching you with big brown eyes, is the black dog from the mine office.

You turn to look at Mr. Grimble.

"Carbon's had a hard day," he says. "Out in the world, savin' people from themselves." He winks at you and whispers, "Can't have visitors gettin' sent home before summer's over!"

The End

110

Things are working out exactly as you planned. The truck pulls over, and you hear Mac unlatching the back. When the door swings open, you leap out at Mac, knocking him to the ground. Roderick grabs Chuck's rifle and holds it on the pair while he tells you how to operate the two-way radio.

The Provincial Police arrive quickly.

"I owe you my life," Roderick says to you later. "Thanks."

"You're welcome," you say. "But I've got a favor to ask you. You lay off Gram about that tax bill. You know she'll pay."

Roderick grins. "Don't worry about it, kid," he says. "You made a thousand bucks today. That's the reward for the hijackers. Enough to pay your gram's taxes and your trespassing fine."

"What?" you yell.

"Twenty bucks for trespassing on the Anchor," Roderick says. "The law is the law. Come on, I'll buy you a milk shake."

The End

But you never reach the gondola. In your haste your foot catches on the rim of the tracks. You stumble and fall. The explosion lights up the tunnel just long enough for you to see the veined quartz clearly.

Gold! You've found the gold!

And now you're buried with it.

The End

The explosion is deafening. As the walls cave in on you and Roderick, his statement about the gold echoes through your head.

There's only one problem. The rest of his life is over.

And so is yours.

The End

ABOUT THE AUTHOR

LOUISE MUNRO FOLEY is the author of many books for young readers, including *The Lost Tribe, The Mystery of the Highland Crest,* and *The Mystery of Echo Lodge* in the Choose Your Own Adventure series. She has also written a newspaper column, and her articles have appeared in the *Christian Science Monitor, The Horn Book,* and *Writer's Digest.* Ms. Foley has won several national awards for writing and editing. In addition to writing, she has hosted shows on radio and television in the United States and Canada. A native of Toronto, Ontario, Canada, Ms. Foley now lives in Sacramento, California. She has two sons.

ABOUT THE ILLUSTRATOR

LESLIE MORRILL is a designer and illustrator whose work has won him numerous awards. He has illustrated over thirty books for children, including the Bantam Classics edition of *The Wind in the Willows;* for the Bantam Skylark Choose Your Own Adventure series, *Indian Trail* and *Mona Is Missing;* and for the Choose Your Own Adventure series, *Lost on the Amazon* and *Mountain Survival.* His work has also appeared frequently in *Cricket* magazine. A graduate of the Boston Museum School of Fine Arts, Mr. Morrill lives near Boston, Massachusetts.

Special Offer
Buy a Bantam Book
for only 50¢.

Now you can have an up-to-date listing of Bantam's hundreds of titles plus take advantage of our unique and exciting bonus book offer. A special offer which gives you the opportunity to purchase a Bantam book for only 50¢. Here's how!

By ordering any five books at the regular price per order, you can also choose any other single book listed (up to a $4.95 value) for just 50¢. Some restrictions do apply, but for further details why not send for Bantam's listing of titles today!

Just send us your name and address and we will send you a catalog!